S0-DQQ-389

THE SKY'S THE LIMIT

SET GOALS

BY SUSANNE M. BUSHMAN

BLUE OWL
BOOKS

TIPS FOR CAREGIVERS

Social and emotional learning (SEL) helps children manage emotions, learn how to feel empathy, create and achieve goals, and make good decisions. Strong lessons and support in SEL will help children establish positive habits in communication, cooperation, and decision-making. By incorporating SEL in early reading, children will be better equipped to build confidence and foster positive peer networks.

BEFORE READING

Talk to the reader about setting goals. Explain that goals help us achieve things.

Discuss: What would you like to achieve? What have you done to try to achieve it already? What more could you do?

AFTER READING

Talk to the reader about a goal he or she would like to set to achieve something.

Discuss: Is the goal realistic? Is it specific? How will you measure if you've achieved your goal? What is your deadline for the goal? Who could you ask for help with your goal?

SEL GOAL

Some students may struggle with self-management, making it hard to meet goals. They may not be able to successfully regulate their emotions, thoughts, and behaviors. Help readers develop these self-management skills. Help them learn to stop and think about their feelings. How can they manage stress? What do they need to do to control impulses? How can they motivate themselves? Discuss how learning to do these things can help them meet goals.

TABLE OF CONTENTS

CHAPTER 1

TURN DREAMS INTO GOALS

What are your dreams? Maybe you want to be a doctor when you grow up. You might want to play on your school's baseball team. **Goals** can help you make those things happen!

A goal is something you work to make happen. Goals can be things you want to learn. Or they can be something you want to do. Goals can also be about your **mindset**. Your goal could be to become more positive!

harmonica

Setting goals can be fun! It also teaches you to work hard. Maybe you want to learn to play your favorite song on a harmonica. It takes a long time, but you finally do it! You feel proud. Reaching goals makes you feel good about yourself.

CHAPTER 2

SETTING GREAT GOALS

How do you make a good goal? Choose something important to you! Maybe you want to make new friends. You are **motivated**! This is a good goal.

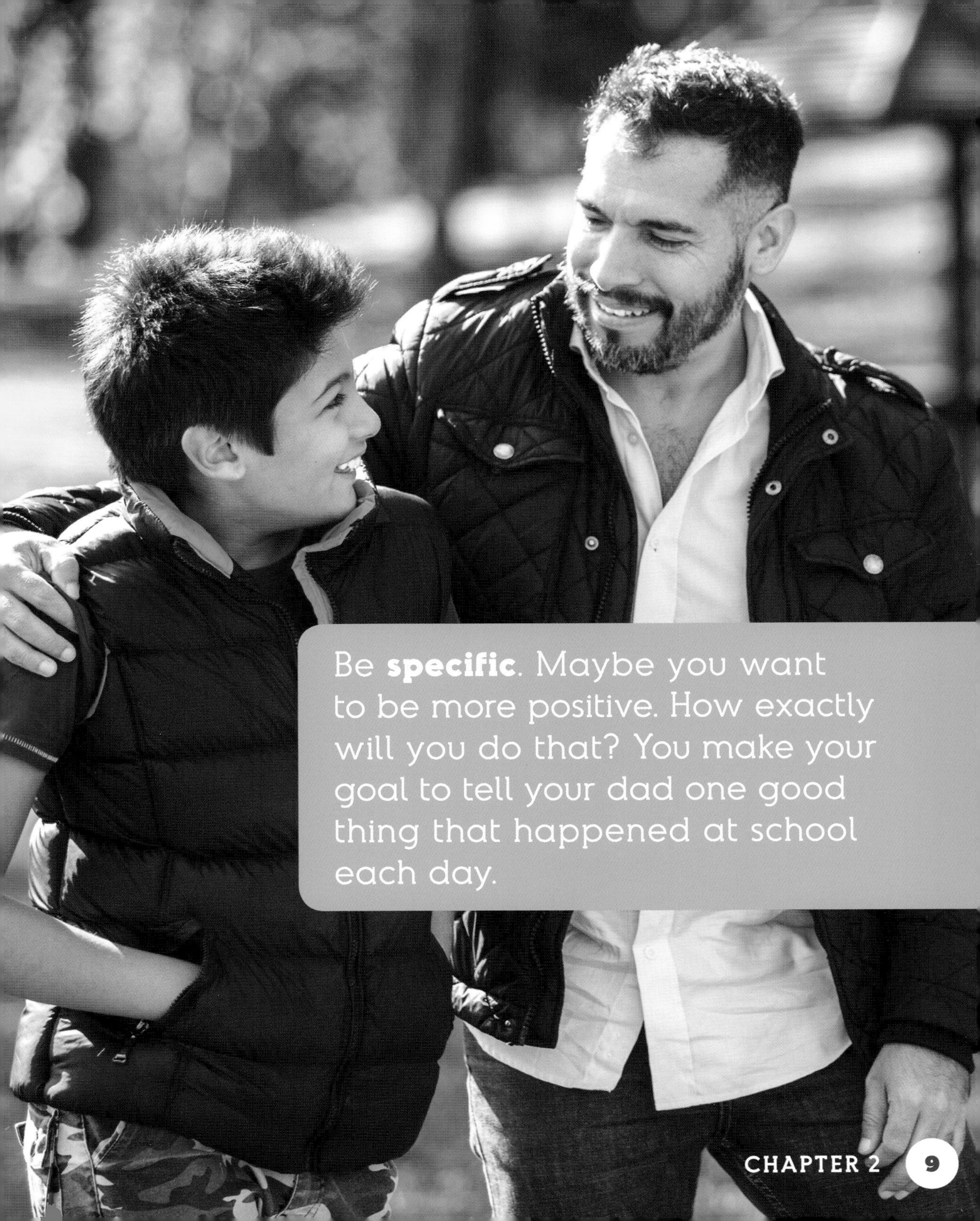

Be **specific**. Maybe you want to be more positive. How exactly will you do that? You make your goal to tell your dad one good thing that happened at school each day.

Start small! Make sure your goals are **achievable**. Don't take on too much too quickly. Maybe you want to write a story. But you've never done it before. Don't make your goal to write 100 pages. Start with 10.

Maybe your goal is to become an astronaut one day. Make a goal for this week. It could be to get a good grade on your science test! Breaking down big goals can help you achieve them!

Breaking goals down into steps will also help you measure your **progress**. Maybe you want to save money for a new game. You come up with ideas to make money. You have a lemonade stand and bake sale. How much more money do you need? You could help a neighbor with yard work. What else could you do?

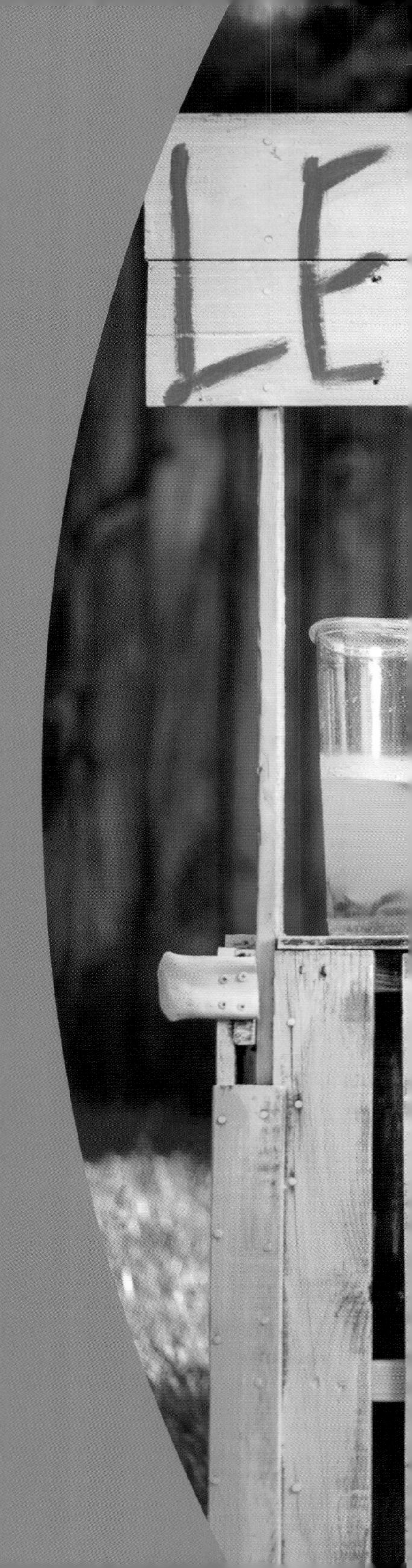

ONADE + BAKE
SALE

Set a **deadline**. Giving yourself a timeframe can help. Maybe your grandma taught you to knit. You want to use your new skill to make her a scarf. You can set a deadline! You will finish the scarf before she visits again in 4 weeks.

SMART GOALS

Use the letters S-M-A-R-T to remember how to make a good goal. What do they stand for?

S: Specific
M: Measurable
A: Achievable
R: **Relevant**
T: Time-specific

CHAPTER 3

WORKING HARD

Getting to your goal can be hard! **Setbacks** are normal. Keep trying. Remember, if you give up, you cannot meet your goal.

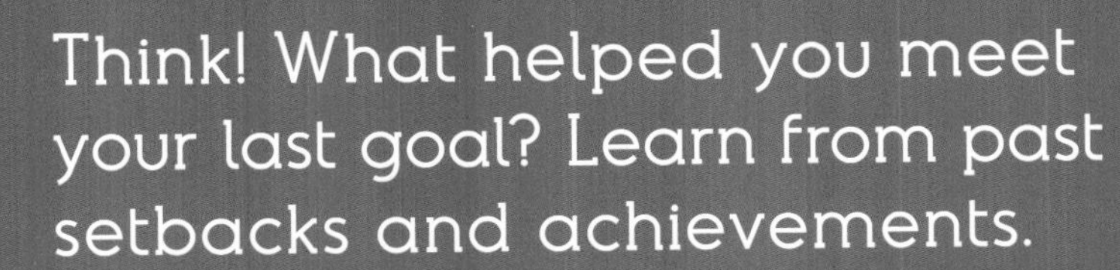
Think! What helped you meet your last goal? Learn from past setbacks and achievements.

It's OK to ask for help with your goal. Be sure to ask people you trust. Having a **network** can make goals easier. People in your network are there to help you. Maybe your goal is to do a **mindfulness** activity each day. It is hard. Your mom **encourages** you. She does it with you.

TRY SOMETHING NEW

Goals are great ways to try new things. Make it your goal to branch out and do something you've never done before.

After you meet your goal, take time to **reflect**. What was hard about meeting your goal? What helped you succeed? Think about how you can achieve your next goal. Writing about it in a journal can be a good way to reflect.

Setting goals helps us achieve our dreams! It helps us improve our lives. What goals will you set?

WHAT'S IMPORTANT?

Many goals are based on your **values**. Think about what you care about. Set goals that connect to those things. **Focus** on your own goals. They might be different from someone else's goals!

CHOOL
ECTION
LOPEZ
FOR
ESIDENT!

GOALS AND TOOLS

GROW WITH GOALS

Achieving goals can be hard. But it makes us feel good about ourselves! We can work on setting better goals for ourselves.

Goal: Reflect on your dreams. What do you want to do one day? What goals can you set to get there?

Goal: Create a goal ladder! Draw a ladder on a piece of paper. Write down your goal on the top step. Then write all the steps you have to take to achieve your goal below it. Draw a star by each step when you complete it!

Goal: Identify your network! Who could help you meet your goals? Do they have goals that you could help them meet?

WRITING REFLECTION

Reflecting on past goals can help you make better goals in the future.

1. What is a recent goal you set?
2. Were you successful in achieving it?
3. If you were, how did you do it? If not, what could you have done differently to achieve your goal?

GLOSSARY

achievable
Able to be done successfully after making an effort.

deadline
A time when something must be finished.

encourages
Gives someone confidence, usually by using praise and support.

focus
To concentrate on something.

goals
Things that you aim to do.

mindfulness
A mentality achieved by focusing on the present moment and calmly recognizing and accepting your feelings, thoughts, and sensations.

mindset
Mental attitude.

motivated
Encouraged by someone or something to do something or to want to do something.

network
An interconnected group of people.

progress
Forward movement or improvement.

reflect
To think carefully or seriously about something.

relevant
Concerned with or connected to something.

setbacks
Problems that delay you or keep you from making progress.

specific
Precise, definite, or of a particular kind.

values
A person's principles of behavior and beliefs about what is important in life.

TO LEARN MORE

Finding more information is as easy as 1, 2, 3.

1. Go to www.factsurfer.com
2. Enter "**setgoals**" into the search box.
3. Choose your cover to see a list of websites.

INDEX

This edition is co-published by agreement between Jump! and World Book, Inc.

Jump!, 5357 Penn Avenue South, Minneapolis, MN 55419, www.jumplibrary.com

World Book, Inc., 180 North LaSalle Street, Suite 900, Chicago, IL 60601, www.worldbook.com

Library of Congress Cataloging-in-Publication Data

Names: Bushman, Susanne M., 1994– author.
Title: Set goals / by Susanne M. Bushman.
Description: Blue owl books. | Minneapolis : Jump!, Inc., 2020.
Series: The sky's the limit | Includes index.
Audience: Ages 7–10. | Audience: Grades 2–3.
Identifiers: LCCN 2019028757 (print)
Jump! ISBN 9781645272052 (hardcover)
World Book ISBN 9780716638797 (hardcover)
Subjects: LCSH: Goal (Psychology)–Juvenile literature.
Classification: LCC BF505.G6 .B87 2020 (print) | DDC 153.8–dc23
LC record available at https://lccn.loc.gov/2019028757

Editor: Jenna Trnka
Designer: Molly Ballanger

Photo Credits: antoniodiaz/Shutterstock, cover, 10–11; Viacheslav Nikolaenko/Shutterstock, 1 (foreground); EFKS/Shutterstock, 1 (background); Pineapple Studio/Shutterstock, 3; PeopleImages/iStock, 4; Joos Mind/Getty, 5; Jose Luis Pelaez Inc/Getty, 6–7, 14–15; Veronica Louro/Shutterstock, 8; Sladic/iStock, 9; Roberto A Sanchez/iStock, 12–13; In Green/Shutterstock, 16; Blur Life 1975/Shutterstock, 17 (background); sharpner/Shutterstock, 17 (foreground); triloks/iStock, 18–19; Chris Clinton/Getty, 20–21.

Printed in the United States of America at Corporate Graphics in North Mankato, Minnesota.